DEC. 1 7 1990	DATE DUE	
DEC. 2 0 1990	SEP. 2 4 1992	OCT 1 2 1995
JAN. 1 0 1991	OCT. 1 2 1992	
FEB. 7 1991	OCT 3 6 1993	NOV 1 6 2004
FEB. 2 8 1991	1994	
MAR. 1 8 1991	JAN 2	MAY 8 2006
JUN. 6 1991	MAR 3 1994	JUN 0 6 2006
JUL. 1 1 1991	MAY 1 9 1994	JUN 2 3 2006
SEP. 2 6 1991	SEP 2 7 1994	MAR 1 1 2008
FEB. 2 7 1992	OCT 1 8 1994	MAY 2 9 2015
AUS. 2 0 1992	FEB 2 8 1995	MAR 1 6 2019
SEP. 7 1992	SEP 2 8 1995	

E
Cas
a

Caseley, Judith
    Apple pie and onions.

JUDITH CASELEY

Apple Pie and Onions

Greenwillow Books New York

Watercolor paints and colored pencils were used for the full-color art. The typeface is ITC Cheltenham.

Library of Congress Cataloging-in-Publication Data
Caseley, Judith.
Apple pie and onions.
Summary: Although she is embarrassed when her
grandmother reminisces with an old friend in
public, Rebecca loves her and enjoys hearing
stories about her grandmother's life in America
when she first came from Russia.
[1. Grandmothers—Fiction.
2. Russian Americans—Fiction.
3. Emigration and immigration—Fiction]
I. Title.
PZ7.C2677Ap 1987   [E]   86-9804
ISBN 0-688-06762-X
ISBN 0-688-06763-8 (lib. bdg.)

FOR GRANDMA REBECCA
AND HER SISTERS AND BROTHER,
WITH LOVE

Rebecca loved to visit Grandma's apartment.

"You'll sleep with Grandma in the big bed," Grandma always said.

Grandma's bed was different from Mama's. It had lots of fancy pillows, and there was a knitted blanket at the foot.

"It's from the old country," said Grandma.

Grandma's bathroom was different, too. It had a big bathtub
on feet with claws. On the shelves there were boxes and boxes
of powders and perfumes, and a bowl of rose petals.
Grandma gave Rebecca her own towel and said, "We'll make
an apple pie today. But first we'll go to the market."

Grandma put on her coat with the fake diamond pin on it.

She pinned one on Rebecca's jacket, too. Then they wheeled

the shopping basket out the door.

They stopped at the butcher's first.

"Hello, Max," said Grandma. "Some soup bones and a piece

of brisket, please."

"Hello, Mary," said the old man. "How's the arthritis?"

When they got outside Rebecca said, "Do you know him,

Grandma?"

Grandma smiled. "Many years ago, he wanted to marry your Aunt Bertha," she said. "But no matter how he washed, Bertha said he smelled like meat. And she wouldn't marry him."

"Who did she marry?" asked Rebecca.

"Your Uncle Dave," said Grandma. "He owned a bakery, and Bertha said he smelled like fresh bread."

They came to the fruit market. Grandma bought a bunch of bananas, and an apple for Rebecca.

"When I was a little girl," said Grandma, "I came here with my mother and sisters on a big boat from Russia. On the boat a nice lady gave me a banana. I had never seen one before. I tried to eat it, skin and all."

Rebecca and Grandma laughed.

"I told my sisters that America had terrible food, if it was anything like bananas," said Grandma.

They walked some more. It was warm outside.

"Papa brought us to a big city with no trees or fresh air.
At night it was so hot we couldn't sleep."

"Didn't you have air-conditioning?" asked Rebecca.

"No," said Grandma. "No one did in those days. Papa
pulled the mattresses out onto the fire escape and we
slept outside. It was nice and cool."

Suddenly, Grandma gave a shout. She ran up to an old lady in a wheelchair and cried, "Hattie! My old friend Hattie!" Hattie and Grandma laughed and shouted, and Grandma talked louder and louder and faster and faster in a foreign language. Everybody watched Grandma and Hattie.

Rebecca moved away. She looked at the ground. She looked at the sky. She made believe she didn't know Grandma.

Grandma said goodbye to Hattie. She came over and hugged Rebecca.

"We were in school together," she said. "And we didn't speak any English, so we talked in Yiddish, until the teacher shut me in the cloakroom. When she opened the door I was sound asleep."

Rebecca turned away from Grandma.

"Please, Grandma," she said. "No more stories."

Grandma took Rebecca's hand. They walked a little.

"Did your old Grandma embarrass you back there, shouting her head off in the market?" she asked.

Rebecca kicked the ground. She sat down on a bench. She didn't answer.

Grandma sat down next to her.

"I'd like to tell you one more story," she said.

"When I was your age, my father met me at school on the very last day and took me home on the train. I was wearing my best white dress, and a ribbon in my hair," said Grandma. "My father was wearing his dirty work clothes. He was carrying a sack of onions and a bag of potatoes."

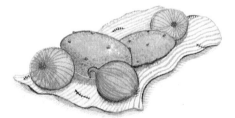

Rebecca looked up at Grandma.

"Did you feel funny?" asked Rebecca.

"Of course," said Grandma. "Everyone else was all dressed up. So I moved one seat away and pretended I didn't know my own papa."

"What happened?" asked Rebecca.

"When we got home," said Grandma, "Papa kissed me and we drank tea together. And Mama made a stew with the onions."

Grandma and Rebecca went home. Grandma put away the groceries and said, "I'm thirsty from all that talking."

"Can we have tea together," said Rebecca, "like you and your papa did?"

Grandma kissed Rebecca and filled up the kettle.

"Tea with lemon in a glass," said Grandma.

After their tea Grandma made the dough for the apple pie.

Rebecca washed the apples, and Grandma sliced them.

When the apples were covered with pie crust Grandma said,

"You can prick the dough."

"All right," said Rebecca, "but don't look."

After supper Rebecca put the pie on the table.

"I love you, Grandma," she said.

"That's just what you wrote on the pie," cried Grandma.

"It's much too beautiful to eat."

Rebecca smiled at Grandma. And then they cut the pie...

and ate it .